Dear Parents and Educators,

Welcome to Penguin Young Readers! As par__
know that each child develops at __
speech, critical thinking, and, of
Readers recognizes this fact. As __
book is assigned a traditional ec
Guided Reading Level (A–P). Bc
the right book for your child. Ple
for specific leveling information
esteemed authors and illustrato__,
fascinating nonfiction, and more!

Muddy, Mud, Bud

LEVEL 1

GUIDED READING LEVEL **D**

This book is perfect for an **Emergent Reader** who:
- can read in a left-to-right and top-to-bottom progression;
- can recognize some beginning and ending letter sounds;
- can use picture clues to help tell the story; and
- can understand the basic plot and sequence of simple stories.

Here are some **activities** you can do during and after reading this book:
- Picture Clues: Use the pictures to tell the story. Have the child go through the book and retell the story just by looking at the pictures.
- Sight Words: Sight words are frequently used words that readers must know instantly, just by looking at them. Knowing these words on sight helps children develop into efficient readers. As you read the story, have the child point out the sight words below.

am	be	good	no	this
are	but	must	now	want

Remember, sharing the love of reading with a child is the best gift you can give!

—Bonnie Bader, EdM
 Penguin Young Readers program

*Penguin Young Readers are leveled by independent reviewers applying the standards developed by Irene Fountas and Gay Su Pinnell in *Matching Books to Readers: Using Leveled Books in Guided Reading*, Heinemann, 1999.

For Andrea Cascardi,
agent and editor extraordinaire—PL

To my parents for always letting me get
muddy, but never too muddy!—CA

PENGUIN YOUNG READERS
Published by the Penguin Group
Penguin Group (USA) LLC, 375 Hudson Street, New York, New York 10014, USA

USA | Canada | UK | Ireland | Australia | New Zealand | India | South Africa | China

penguin.com
A Penguin Random House Company

Text copyright © 2014 by Patricia Lakin. Illustrations copyright © 2014 by Penguin Group (USA) LLC.
Published by Penguin Young Readers, an imprint of Penguin Group (USA) LLC,
345 Hudson Street, New York, New York 10014.
Manufactured in China.

Library of Congress Cataloging-in-Publication Data is available.

ISBN 978-0-448-47989-7 (pbk)   10 9 8 7 6 5 4 3 2
ISBN 978-0-448-47990-3 (hc)   10 9 8 7 6 5 4 3 2 1

Muddy, Mud, Bud

by Patricia Lakin
illustrated by Cale Atkinson

Penguin Young Readers
An Imprint of Penguin Group (USA) LLC

I like to be muddy.

It makes me look good.

Splish! Splash!

I jump in the mud.

Rub-a-dub-dub.

I rub on the mud.

But I want more mud!

Scrub-a-dub-dub.

I scrub on the mud.

I must have

more mud.

There must be mud in there.

Here I go.

Splish! Splash!

I am wet.

I am wet with

muddy, mud, mud.

Rub-a-dub-dub.

Rub on the mud.

Scrub-a-dub-dub.

Scrub on the mud.

I am Muddy, Mud, Bud.

No! This is not mud.

These are suds.

I am wet.

And I am clean!

I am not Muddy, Mud, Bud.

I must have more mud!

There must be mud there.

I tip and I spill.

Muddy, mud, mud.

30

Rub-a-dub-dub.

Scrub-a-dub-dub.

Now I am Muddy, Mud, Bud!